The Great Fire

Born in Wolverhampton, Andrew moved to Shropshire at the age of five. His career in retail training took him to Surrey and Gloucestershire before settling back in Ludlow, Shropshire. He currently works as a Quality Auditor for a large work based training provider.

Andrew has been writing poetry and short stories since the age of fifteen, and "The Great Fire" is Andrew's first illustrated children's book to be published.

Andrew lives with his partner, Sarah of three years and her two children, Hayley and Adam.

The Great Fire

Andrew Nicholls

The Great Fire

Olympia Publishers
London

www.olympiapublishers.com
OLYMPIA PAPERBACK EDITION

Copyright © Andrew Nicholls 2010

The right of Andrew Nicholls to be identified as author of this work has been asserted in accordance with sections 77 and 78 of the Copyright, Designs and Patents Act 1988.

All Rights Reserved

No reproduction, copy or transmission of this publication may be made without written permission. No paragraph of this publication may be reproduced, copied or transmitted save with the written permission of the publisher, or in accordance with the provisions of the Copyright Act 1956 (as amended).

Any person who does any unauthorized act in relation to this publication may be liable to criminal prosecution and civil claims for damage.

A CIP catalogue record for this title is available from the British Library.

ISBN: 978-1-848973-050-2

This is a work of fiction.
Names, characters, places and incidents originate from the writer's imagination. Any resemblance to actual persons, living or dead, is purely coincidental.

First Published in 2010

Olympia Publishers
60 Cannon Street
London
EC4N 6NP

Printed in Great Britain

Dedication

To my folks, who always encouraged me to chase my dreams.
And to Sarah, who dreamt it all up in the first place.

Acknowledgments

Thanks go to my wonderful parents and "big sis" who always believed in me and gave all the support imaginable. My partner, Sarah, and her two children who have taught me patience, how to laugh at life and the secrets to retaining my youth! Finally, to Stu, lifelong friend and a monster on the guitar! He will always play the music I most want to listen to. Thanks guys!

Contents

The start of it all   15

Harry's Tale   19

   Breadcrumbs   21
   Escape from the kitchen   24
   Up in smoke!   29
   Waking the neighbours   31
   Harry heads north   33
   The burning house   35
   A trip through the city   43

Chester's Adventures   49

   The last good night's sleep   51
   Up to the Tower   53
   Boating on the Thames   55
   Cat overboard!   56
   Out of the frying pan…   61
   Running from the dogs   65
   No way out!   69

Sally's Story — 73

    The calm before the storm — 75
    Hiding in the Tower — 78
    The Molten River — 83
    Look out below! — 87
    Horse play! — 91
    Clinging by a thread — 93

The end of it all — 97

    The ruined Cathedral — 100
    A friendly face — 105
    A home at last — 109

The start of it all

The three animals sat on the hill and watched their city burn. Great plumes of smoke rose up from the fiery glow that was once their home. The smoke rose up and up into the cloudy sky as the sun began to set. The darkness began to envelop the hill, giving an eerie glow that made Harry shudder as he watched the flames consume the city.

They weren't watching the fire alone. A large number of people had come up to Parliament Hill to watch, in safety, the destruction of London. No one spoke. It was as if there was nothing left to say, nothing left to do but to watch and wait.

The people didn't seem to notice the three animals amongst them, or chose to ignore them in light of the devastation that had befallen the city.

"What are we going to do now?" whispered Harry to his two companions. He had just lost his house and was unsure if all of his family made it from the fire. The two animals just shook their heads and turned back to look at the distant glow of the fire.

Harry wasn't looking his best. Usually light brown in colour, the soot had turned the little mouse dirty black, although he still had his little pink nose. His pink feet were covered in mud and he smelt all smoky from the fire that still raged in the city. His friends on the hill, Sally, a brown rat and Chester, a rough looking moggy, hadn't fared much better!

Normally, rats, mice and cats kept themselves to themselves and seldom met up. Indeed, a cat is more likely to hunt and eat rodents than engage in conversation. However these were exceptional circumstances, and now was not the time for fighting.

"We may be here for some time, at least until the fires are out," sighed Harry, wiping soot from his eyes.

"I know what we should do, let's tell each other all about how we got here. I bet all three of us have a story to share!" Chester was right of course. Each had adventures just waiting to be told and as there was nothing else to do except watch their beloved city burn, they agreed. Harry went first. He half closed his eyes, let out a long sigh, and began.

Harry's Tale

Breadcrumbs

"The day was like any other as I remember. I had woken in the early morning and took a walk around the house, looking for a snack. The baker, Thomas, had started the ovens on the previous day as usual and I can honestly say that the smell of freshly baking bread sets my tummy rumbling! There were always crumbs on the floor around the hearth and that day was no exception. This is the main reason that I moved into the bakery from my family home up the street. There is, or I should say, was a crack in the wall right by the oven and it made a great home. Anyway, I was gathering the bread crumbs up that morning when I heard footsteps coming down the stairs. It wasn't the baker but his apprentice. You should hear the baker cursing at him! I wouldn't like to work for him, I know that much!

"He sounds a horrible man, why is he so horrible to his workers?" inquired Sally, shaking her little brown head.

"He has a lot of pressure to make bread. He is the king's baker you see," replied Harry, proudly. He had always been proud of the place he lived having a royal connection.

"Anyway, I carried on gathering the breadcrumbs when I noticed something unusual. The oven was still hot! Usually it stays warm into the early hours of the morning even though it is put out at the end of each day, but that morning, it was still lit!! Not only that but looking up to the ceiling I could see smoke swirling around. This was definitely not usual. And then... I saw the flames.

"Flames, Harry! I have seen more than enough of them to last me a lifetime!" Chester shuddered at the thought and gestured Harry to continue.

"The nearby log pile had caught fire and was crackling with the flames that licked up to touch the ceiling as I watched. I couldn't move! I had never seen such a sight outside of the hearths in the bakery. Scared was not the word. I was terrified!

"I thought of trying to put out the flames but knew I couldn't. I am far too small to carry large amounts of water around. Luckily, the baker's apprentice was bigger! I heard him shriek with alarm as I finally managed to pull myself together and bolt under the large wooden table in the centre of the room. He grabbed a bucket from the corner of the room and ran to get the water with which he would, hopefully, douse the flames. He was only gone out of the room for a minute but by then it was too late. The fire had spread and half of the kitchen was ablaze. The smoke was getting thicker and thicker and I had to get out. The apprentice had returned but must have realised he was too late. I remember he started shouting for the baker to get out of the house as he ran out of the kitchen, pulling the door shut behind him. I ran as fast as I could but I was too slow, and the door shut fast. I was trapped in the burning kitchen with no way out!!

"Oh Harry! Whatever did you do? How on earth did you get out of the kitchen?" gasped Sally in alarm. She had been listening intently to every word that Harry had said, clasping and unclasping her paws at the point the fire started to when the door had closed on Harry.

"Yes Harry, tell us how to goodness you escaped!" cried Chester. He too had been listening to Harry with wide green eyes, letting his tail flick wildly as the story progressed.

"Well it wasn't easy I can tell you. This is what I did." Harry rubbed his nose with a little pink paw, leaving a sooty mark on the tip. Sniffing and with a twitch of his long white whiskers, Harry continued.

Escape from the kitchen

"I have to admit to panicking at this point. There was a tiny gap under the door but try as I might I couldn't possibly squeeze through. I tried to dig the floor to make a bigger gap but my little paws weren't strong enough. The smoke was getting thicker and thicker. I could hardly breathe and the heat of the fire became unbearable. And then I spied the window! It was open, just a fraction. No man could have squeezed through but maybe a mouse?

"Yes Harry, the window. You could squeeze through most things being so tiny I bet", whispered Sally and Chester nodded in agreement; secretly thanking his lucky stars it hadn't been him in that room.

"So did you jump up and out Harry? Tell us, tell us how you freed yourself". Harry duly told them and continued his story.

"It was too high! There was no way to reach the window from the floor. My escape was so near and yet so very far away. It was then, through the smoke, that I noticed the broom leaning on the table in the middle of the kitchen. If I could push it off it would fall against the window, providing the perfect bridge for a small mouse to climb across!! If I could push it!

"Quickly I ran across the floor to the nearest leg of the table. I have often climbed up to get the warm, freshly baked bread so knew this would be easy enough. Despite the smoke and flames I clambered up and scrambled onto the table top, coughing and spluttering so much as I did so. It was really, really smoky on the high table. I could barely see the broom handle leaning on the edge just a few mouse steps away. I needed a run up so I started at the far end of the table, took a deep breath and ran at the broom!

"I leapt onto the handle, digging my claws in and found it was moving. I clung on tight as it moved away from the table. It seemed to balance upright and I had a horrible feeling that it was going to topple back, that I wasn't heavy enough to push it all the way. After what seemed an eternity, the broom continued on its journey to the window. It hit with such force that the top of the broom smashed straight through a small pane, sending the glass crashing to the floor of the street below.

"You were lucky not to cut your paws with all the glass around!"

"I know Sally, I had to be careful but I could smell the fresh air gushing in and I didn't hesitate in climbing up the broom and out, down the brickwork and across the street where I turned to face my home. What a sight to see!"

Up in smoke!

"What was it you saw Harry? Tell us please!" Chester was wide eyed and itching to know what sight could be seen. Harry quickly explained.

"The cold air from the broken window seemed to have given more life to the fire and both the table and broom were well alight. I had escaped by mere seconds and this thought made me shudder (and, if I'm honest, still does). Smoke was billowing out of the broken window and the street was lit with an orange glow that moved and flickered as if alive. The entire downstairs was well alight, not just the kitchen. Something caught my attention higher up and a window suddenly opened. I saw the baker and his family begin to clamber out of the upstairs bedroom window, followed by the apprentice. They had no choice; they had become trapped by the fire below. There were screams and shouts, people began to emerge from their houses to look at the devastation unfolding before them. Thomas jumped to the roof of the next house along in Pudding Lane, followed closely by his family. They had escaped too. Huddling together they started shouting for their maid to leave the house. I never saw her jump so I don't know what happened to her.

"The flames began to lick the roof and smoke could clearly be seen drifting slowly up into the night sky. A stiff wind was blowing and I remember shrinking back into the doorway of the house opposite, trying to stay out of the way of the heat from the flames and the drifting smoke. Another shout was heard, this time from the house adjoining the bakery. The flames from the roof were spreading over to the house. I noticed, with horror that the roof had caught fire. It was being consumed with such ferocity that a horrible thought occurred to me. The houses were built so close together, what was to stop the fire spreading to each and every house in the street? And who lived at the end of the street? My family! I had to warn them. Without hesitation, I ran down the middle of the street to my parents' home."

Waking the neighbours

Harry paused in his story telling to look again at the fire engulfing London. Even from this distance, the flames could still be seen and a distant crackling, shouting and disturbance could be heard, spoiling the quiet of the night. Sally and Chester waited patiently for the little mouse to carry on. After a few more moments, Harry continued.

"The house was still in darkness when I arrived, puffing and panting from the long run I had just completed. All was quiet but, even then, the shouts from further up the street were beginning to penetrate the stillness of the early morning gloom. I reached the drainpipe and clambered up until I reached the broken part. Once inside the pipe I made my way up until I reached the crack in the wall of the house. I went inside and ran straight across the first floor living room to the wall by the hearth. I crept into the hole in the wall and ran to my parents who were asleep curled up in a ball. They were rather surprised to see me!

"Harry, what on earth are you doing creeping around at this time in the morning?" my Mother had cried, in obvious alarm at being woken so suddenly by her youngest son. I had no time to apologise for this but knew we only had a short amount of time.

"I quickly told my terrible tale and saw a change come over them the instant they heard of the spreading fire. I helped them gather up a few belongings and we were soon out in the street.

Looking up the street we saw the flames and smoke, alarmingly closer than before and it had spread to both sides. We could all feel the heat and clearly hear the crackling of flames devouring the houses just a few doors up from my parent's home.

"We walked quietly up the street getting as close as we dared to the fire. There were lots of people running around, screaming and shouting. No one could put the fire out; it was far too big for that. My parents decided to head for the bridge to cross the river. We have relatives on the other side of the river and they would always welcome us to stop whenever we wished. I knew the wind was blowing that way and tried to explain that the fire would head in that direction. Try as I might they wouldn't listen and begged me to go with them. I couldn't. I had to go up wind and head north. I tried to convince them one last time but they had made their minds up. Sadly I said goodbye and headed up the alley, watching them hurrying the opposite way. This was probably the hardest thing to see during all of these terrible events.

"Oh Harry, have you heard? The bridge caught fire. You were right, Harry you were right".

"I know Sally but I hope my parents crossed before it happened", sighed Harry. There was silence between the three animals. At last, Chester broke the silence.

"Harry, finish the story. How did you get up here?"

Harry heads north

"I knew that I had to get away, and North seemed the best choice. Unless the wind changed of course but there was no sign of that happening. There were people and animals everywhere, Shouts, screams filled the street. People were throwing their belongings into carts or simply bundling them up and fleeing the smoke and flames. I had to keep my wits about me unless I wanted to be squished by the rampaging, scared people. I kept to the houses and ran from house to house, slowly making my way up Gracechurch Street.

As I walked, the fire and smoke receded and at last I remember stopping at the top end of the street and breathing in the London air without coughing (or at least no more than I usually do living here in London)! I spent the afternoon watching the comings and goings of the people, hurrying back and forth with goods and waiting for the fire to stop so I could go back home. By early evening I realised that the fire wasn't yet out and decided to sleep for the night in the nearby house of Mayor Bludworth.

"Wow Harry! I have heard he lives in a very posh place. Was it as beautiful as people make out?"

"Yes, I can honestly say Sally, it was a very beautiful house", acknowledged Harry before continuing the story.

"I squeezed through a small gap at the foot of the front door and snuggled down at the back of a large chair. There was no one else in the house. I don't remember much else that night as I was soon asleep, dreaming of fires, smoke and danger!"

Harry paused at this point, remembering the danger he had been in and, indeed the danger he would face before arriving on Parliament Hill. Harry stood and stretched his legs, flicking his tail relentlessly as he watched the burning before him. Turning to face his companions, he carried on with his story.

The burning house

"I awoke coughing and spluttering. The sunlight shining through the window was being diffused by thick smoke. The fire was spreading and it had reached Gracechurch Street. Once again, I found myself in a house on fire! I quickly noticed that the fire had reached the front door and window. There was no way out of the house that way so I hurried to the back of the house. Again, smoke and fire greeted me, making me step back. I ran out and up the stairs to the first floor. Where could I go?

"I made my way into the Mayor's bedroom which had begun to fill with the smoke that was creeping up the stairs behind me. The bed was next to the window so I climbed up and onto the window sill. The window was ajar but the drop was too great for me to jump without certain injury, if not death! I looked out onto the street. If I could make it I knew I could run to safety. There were people running about panicking. Some were pushing carts piled high with their personal belongings. I decided to jump onto a passing cart to break my fall; it was my only chance. Looking up the street I saw one making its way up, pulled by an old man. He was slow so I felt I had a good chance of making the jump. That's when I heard the bird in the cage.

"Ooh, I like birds! They make such pretty noises". Harry either ignored Sally's comment or didn't hear her as he carried on with his story regardless.

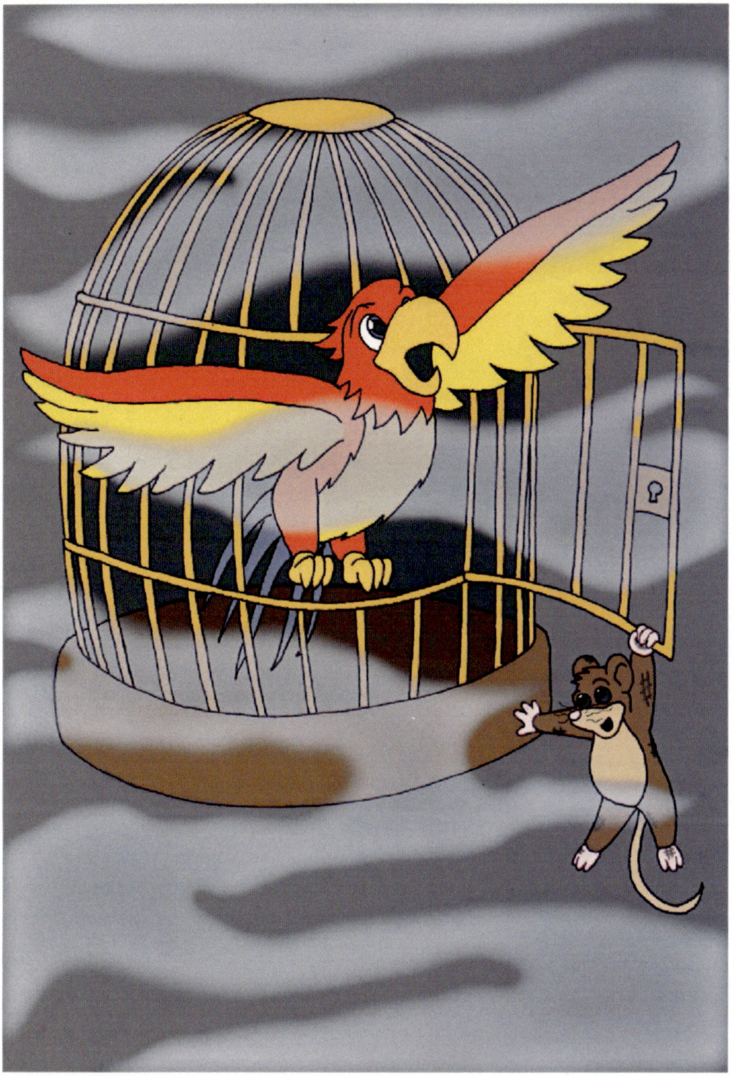

"The bird was pleading with me to let it out of the cage so it could escape from the burning house. I was so close to freedom but looking at the man with the cart I chanced that I had a few moments to spare. I jumped down from the window, across the bed and up to the cage that was perched on the dresser near the door. Smoke was making it difficult to see and I could hear the crackling of fire and the creaking of timbers outside the bedroom. I pulled at the cage door but it wouldn't budge. I nibbled the bars, tasting the cage as I tried to bite through. A combination of the two saw the door give a little. I had succeeded in bending the door just enough for the little bird to squeeze through. He flew out of the window and was gone, shouting his thank you to me as he went.

"Harry, you are such a hero. I don't know if I would have gone back for a bird, I usually try to eat them anyway!" Chester said, licking his lips as he did so.

"It wasn't a moment too soon either. The bedroom door suddenly burst into flames and the floor of the bedroom began to sag and fall inwards to the room below. I jumped from the dresser straight onto the bed as it too sank through the floor with a groan. I scrambled up the window sill. The old man was passing underneath with his cart and I had no time to think. I jumped!

"I remember hitting the cart with a bang and my front paw throbbed with pain as I landed awkwardly. Nevertheless, I had made it. I looked back at the Mayor's house just in time to see it collapse in on itself and fall in a smoke filled heap. The old man quickened his step and turned into Lombard Street, heading away from the fire.

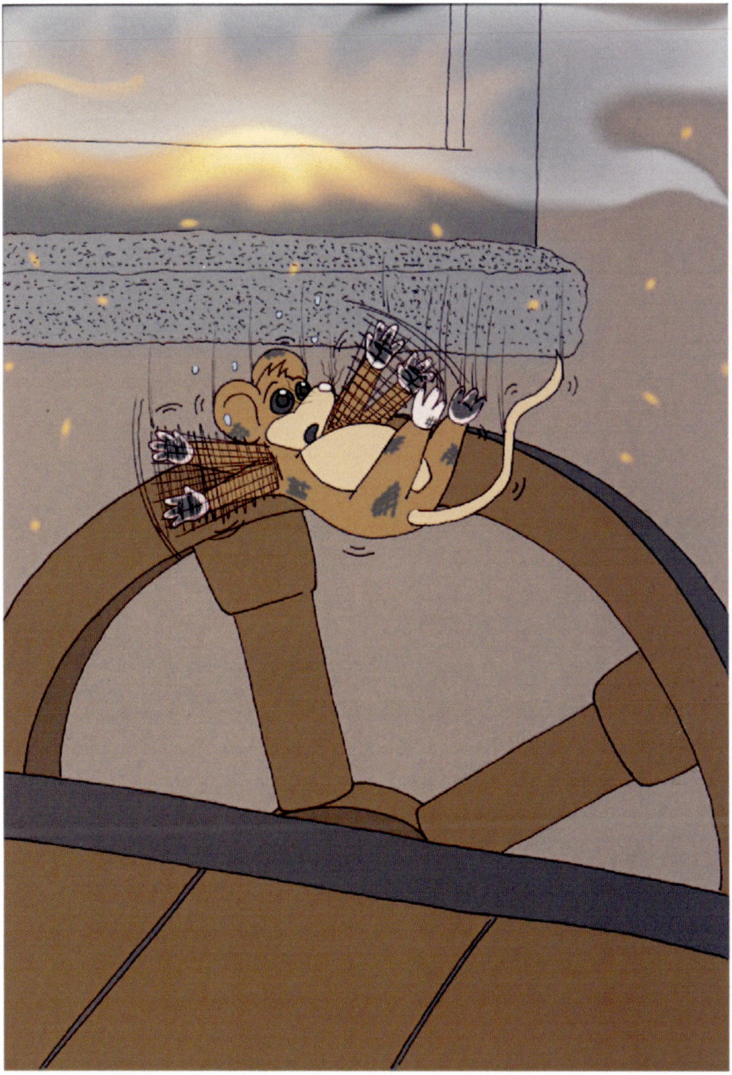

A trip through the city

"We went at quite a pace, certainly quicker than a mouse could have lasted over a period of time. The old man was helped at the end of Lombard Street by another, younger man and together the cart travelled much quicker than before. I hid in an old woollen blanket, peering out at the street before us and being thankful I had escaped not once but twice from the great fire.

"We were travelling through Cheapside on our way to St Paul's when I noticed something out of the corner of my eye. A ginger flash ran from the pavement across the road. I don't know what it was but saw the young man trip on the thing and fall onto the road, letting go of the cart as he did so. The old man moved quicker than I had seen him do all day and, as the cart toppled he grabbed the other handle to steady it. I tried to hold on to the Woollen blanket but lost my grip and fell onto the road, bumping my head in the process.

Harry paused to rub his head thoughtfully before continuing his story to his new found friends. "By the time I had got myself together the men had taken up the cart and walked off. I was back on my own once more. I walked past the great St Paul's Cathedral and prayed that it wouldn't get caught in the fire. I don't think my prayers were answered however."

Sally bowed her head at this point and silently wished for the fire to have never happened.

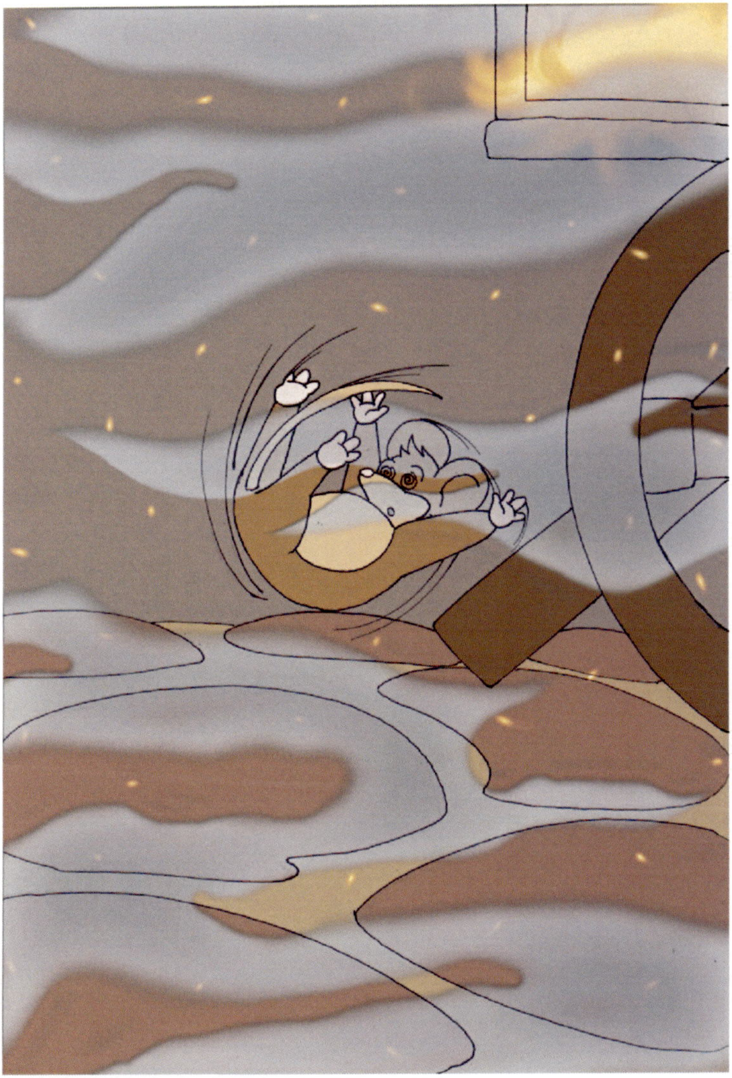

"I travelled on several carts after St Paul's, hiding in the belongings of the homeless until I finally ended up here at Parliament Hill. Everyone seemed confident that the fire would never reach so far.

"And so here I am. I don't know if my parents made it from the fire, or if I can ever return home again. That's my story." Harry sighed and sat down again next to his friends, head bowed and lost in thought.

"Oh Harry, you have been through so much. I can't believe you managed to get so far and escape right from the heart of the fire", whimpered Sally, holding him close to her.

"Its amazing what has happened to you Harry. It's making my story look a bit dull but here goes anyway". Chester cleared his throat, letting out a small meow before he too began his tales of adventure and escape.

Chester's Adventures

The last good night's sleep

"I remember it all so vividly. I have a good memory, you see, due to having to know where the best scraps can be found around the streets where I live. Whose house has a warm, cosy, fire to snuggle next to and whose house to avoid (I don't like being hit with brooms too often)!

"Don't you have a home then, Chester?" asked Sally, amazed (Sally herself has lived all her life in the grand Cathedral in London).

"Not a fixed home, any rate. I like to have several around the town but if I was to choose one it would be the one that Jane lives in."

"Who is Jane? Would I know her?"

"Oh, I doubt you would know her. She is just a maid but has a heart of gold and always lets me stay".

"Anyhow, as I said, I have a very good memory. It all started when I was with Jane at her master's house, Samuel Pepys. I was snoozing by the open hearth as Jane went about her duties, getting ready for the next day's lunch when all of a sudden she stopped and gazed out of the window".

"Can you see that, little cat? Looks like a right good fire over there"; (she didn't know my name). I let out a meow to say I couldn't see anything (although I was rather sleepy) but she was so excited that she went and woke Samuel up. He seemed a little put out about being awoken at such an ungodly hour and I remember him clearly dismissing the fire as a usual sight and that Jane had nothing to worry about.

"Oh Chester, how could he make such a mistake. Look at what the fire has done!" cried Harry shaking his little head in disbelief.

"Yes Harry, but as you know, its not like fires are uncommon here in London. They happen often". And of course, Harry knew that Chester was right about this. He himself had seen numerous fires started in London and never once thought anything would ever come of them. Chester continued. "Samuel seems a fine man so I was happy to take his word for this. I slept well for the rest of the night, I haven't slept well since!"

The three animals were disturbed suddenly on the hill as they were telling their stories by two men arguing. It seemed to be about a cart, laden with goods that had toppled over. The one man was accusing the other of causing the accident. It looked like they were about to come to blows.

"Come on, let's move away. I hate to see fights, especially after all that has happened". Sally was trembling as she said it so Harry put his paw on hers and led her to a spot away from the hustle and bustle of the people on the hill. Once moved, they all curled up and watched the fire consuming the city once more. After a short while, Chester continued.

Up to the Tower

"The next morning Jane was giving me breakfast (rather nice scraps from the night before) when she noticed the fire again. Samuel was told straight away and this time he was more concerned. I felt a bit scared seeing Samuel looking like that. He decided to go to the tower to have a good look. Although I was feeling a bit scared, I decided to go with him. I wanted to see for myself how bad it was getting.

"Chester you are brave, I think I would have stayed at home!" said Sally, staring in admiration at the ginger cat in front of her. Chester just glowed with pride at being called brave!

"We set off to the tower. The son of J Robinson came with us who I have always liked as he sometimes plays with me in the street. I kept back from the people so as not to draw attention to myself. I wasn't officially invited you see! When we finally arrived, I couldn't believe what I saw! The fire was raging and had even reached the bridge. Not all of it was on fire but a lot of it was. There were people running about, screaming and shouting at the tops of their voices. Smoke was filling the houses by the river. I felt so sorry for the people but there was nothing I could do.

"My family were trying to cross the river by that bridge. I don't know if they ever made it". Harry sobbed into his little paws and wished upon wish that his Mom and Dad were with him, safe on the hill.

"Some people did make it across Harry. There's no reason why you're family didn't. Don't worry; I'm sure that they are fine". Chester did his best to reassure Harry before continuing his extraordinary tale.

"Samuel wanted to get closer to the fire, just to see quite how bad it really was. I followed him from the tower as he headed down to the river.

Boating on the Thames

"I don't have very good sea legs and don't really like the water, being a cat and all that! I think I was getting caught up with the adventure of it all as I suddenly decided to sneak into the boat and go for a river trip up the Thames with Samuel. Looking back now, I really wished that I hadn't!!

"The boat was an old rowing boat with a large set of oars and several places to sit. While Samuel was chatting to the boatman, arranging the trip up the river, I slipped onto the boat, finding a place near the back and hid under some old cloth, out of sight.

"I hate water. You wouldn't catch me anywhere near the river!" Harry shook his head and folded his arms in defiance.

"We were soon off and slowly making our way up river. The fire looked even more terrifying nearer and I could clearly see the people running about. A lot were putting their belongings into boats and leaving the banks of the river at an alarming rate. All of a sudden the river was getting decidedly crowded! And that's when it happened

"What was it that happened Chester? Tell us please", cried Sally.

Cat overboard!

"I was looking over the side of the boat at the fire, watching those huge swirls of black smoke rising up into the sky, when I noticed one of the boats laden with furniture, clothes and several people coming alarmingly quickly towards us. There were several shouts of "look out" and our boat turned quickly away from the other vessel. It was a sharp turn which sent me reeling over to the other side of the boat. I clung on desperately to the wooden side of the boat but my claws aren't what they used to be, I felt myself slipping and sliding across the rough wood. Then I was falling! I braced myself and then.... splash!! I landed straight into the water!

"I remember coughing and tasting the awful Thames water. I felt sure that any moment I would be smacked on the head with one of the oars as they were being waved frantically as the boat continued to lurch from side to side. My fur was waterlogged and I began to feel myself sinking down into the murky depths. I don't know whether it was instinct or a long forgotten talent that I used to possess but I began to swim, adopting the stroke popular with the dogs of London (I often watch them in the park, splashing through the ponds with very waggy tails). Through the water and smoke I could just make out the bank of the Thames.

"Again, looking back I most probably should have struck for the opposite bank but it was further and I wasn't confident that I could make it in time. My absence didn't seem to have been noticed as the boat I fell from continued up the Thames, the boat that almost struck us going in the opposite direction, both rowing for all they were worth. I was close to the bank and could hear the crackling of the raging fire which was burning above me over the bank. At last I made it to the shore and clung onto the grassy, muddy bank, digging in with my claws for all I was worth. It seemed to take me an age to get to the top of the bank but at last I had made it and lay, gasping for air. The swim and struggle up the bank had almost done me in!!

Both Sally and Harry were totally engrossed in the story, hugging each other tighter and tighter as Chester recalled the terrifying events that had befallen him.

"And you said you're story wasn't as exciting as mine!" exclaimed Harry, shaking his head in disbelief.

"It's the most exciting story of all!"

"And I wish that it was the end of it. But my adventures had really only just begun. You see, I may have survived the dunking in the Thames, but I was now stood on a muddy bank surrounded by the greatest fire I had ever seen!"

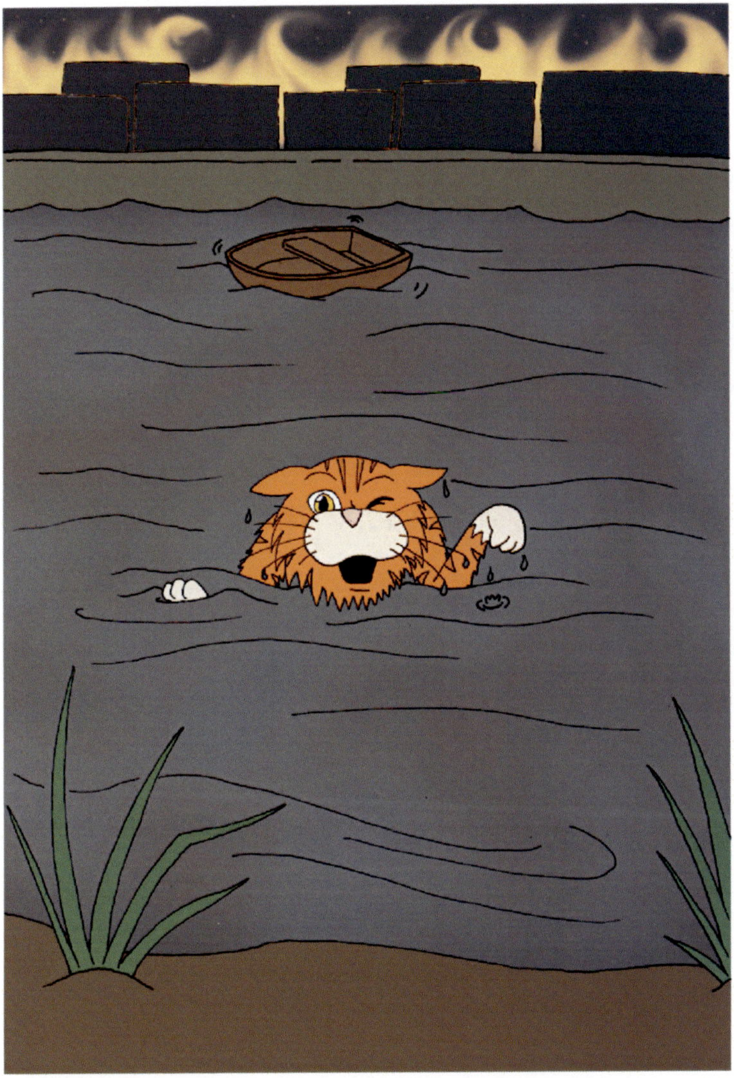

Out of the frying pan......

"The houses closest to the river were burning brightly and a few had already collapsed into a fiery mess. I have to admit to being close to panicking as I had no idea which way to go or how to escape. I ran along the bank looking for a street that led up and away from the river. People were hurrying past with carts, others were just running. I could see pigeons fluttering wildly in the air, some were even on fire!

"That's the most terrible thing I have ever heard!" And with that, Sally held her head in her paws and sobbed her little heart out. Harry was quick to comfort her.

"As I didn't want to share the same fate, I kept running. At last, I saw a street ahead of me, heading up a hill away from the river. There was fire all around it but I had no choice. I plucked up the courage and made a dash for it! I ran up All Hallows Lane, dodging and weaving around the running, screaming people. It was very hot and the smoke stung my eyes, making me blink hard.

"I kept running away from the fires, through Upper Thames Street and onto Queen Street, heading north. At least the heat of the fire had dried me out by now!

"Did you know where you were going Chester?" squeaked Sally.

"I can't say that I did and as I ran onto Cheapside I should have been looking where I was going too!"

"As I ran across the road I suddenly noticed two men pulling a cart quickly up the street. I meowed a warning but they kept coming and one (the younger man) trod on my paw. This sent him stumbling and I noticed the cart toppling as I too fell over, falling end over end until I ended up in a heap in the gutter. Chester looked at his paw and held it, gingerly as he remembered the accident. Harry suddenly seemed to remember something and looked at Chester with a funny expression on his face.

"It was you that tripped up the cart! Chester that was the cart I was hiding in. How strange is that?" Chester looked at Harry and suddenly started to laugh. And then Harry laughed. And then Sally laughed. After all, it was rather funny! After a while, the laughter died down and Chester continued his story.

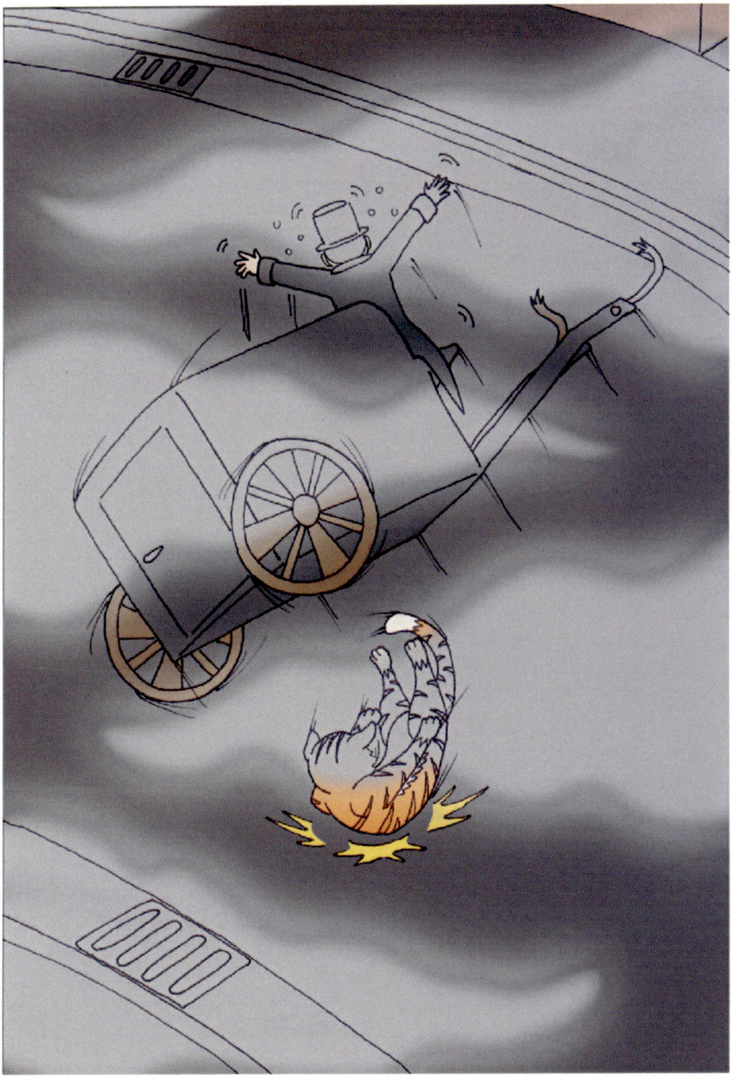

Running from the dogs

"I watched the cart being pulled away into the distance as I lay in the gutter and wondered what to do next. I was wondering this for quite some time when I heard the noise I feared more than anything else in the world. A deep, low growl! Dogs!!

"The mere mention of the dogs sent a shiver down Sally and Harry's spine. Both had had encounters with various dogs and none were particularly pleasant towards them.

"I saw them coming up the street towards me. There were two mangy mutts that clearly lived on the streets. They looked hungry! They broke into a run and I wasn't going to stick around to see if they were friendly or not. Sore paw or no sore paw, I quickly ran up the street away from the dogs. My paw was hurting and I wasn't as fast as I normally am. I could hear them barking and snarling, getting closer and closer. It was at that moment that I knew I couldn't out run them. I would have to try something else!

"I noticed a house up the street which had its door open, just slightly but my sharp eyes spotted it straight away. I got to the door and pushed my head through, then my shoulders, and then I was stuck! The door must have swollen in the heat and was wedged on the floor of the house. I could hear the barking dogs getting nearer and nearer. I pushed and squeezed and wriggled for all I was worth. I was sure the dogs would get to me before I got through when suddenly, pop! I shot through the gap tumbling into the house. And not a moment too soon as looking back at the door I could see the dogs snarling mouths, rows of gleaming teeth and sharp claws on big paws scratching and biting, trying to get in. They were too big to squeeze through the gap. They couldn't get in, but then, I couldn't get out!

"Trapped in a house, I know what that's like", exclaimed Harry shaking his head at the prospect.

"Too true Harry, but I wasn't intending to stay trapped for long, especially as I knew that the fire was almost at the house".

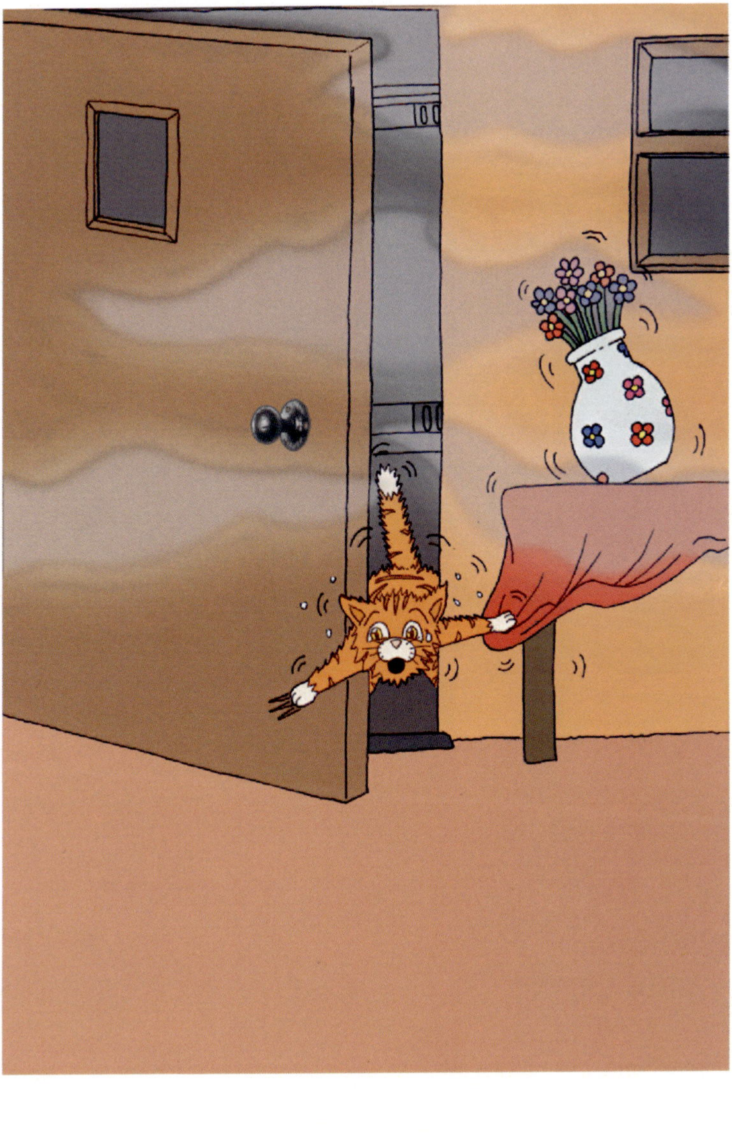

No way out!

"In fact, the house had just caught fire on the roof so I had a bit of time to spare but knew it would catch quickly. I ran to the back of the house, aware of the barking, ravenous dogs at the front who were still trying to get in. The back door was old and worn. A panel was broken and loose and I could see the daylight just beyond the door.

"I started to nibble and scratch the door, chewing off bits and spitting them out behind me. Bit by bit the door came away and a hole in the door began to get bigger and bigger. I briefly stopped to listen to the two dogs again. They were clearly making progress and I could hear splintering of wood. They would soon be in the house with me.

"Hurry, Chester. Hurry and get through the door!" Sally was waving her little paws frantically at Chester, as if it would help him to escape.

"I quickened my work and the door came away more easily. A big crack behind me signified the dogs triumph and I heard the scrabbling of claws on the hall floor as they ran towards me. I ripped off the last piece of door, making the hole big enough for me to squeeze through and so I scrabbled through, pulling my tail around me as the lead dog snapped at it with his big jaws. I was out! The dogs barked and snarled but couldn't get out the tiny hole I had made. Without looking back I ran, back onto the street and continued my journey, travelling north –

West. Looking back at the street I could see the house I had been in consumed in the fire. I couldn't see the dogs anywhere. I doubt they escaped in time.

"From here I ran along Cheapside and passed the glorious St Paul's Cathedral, still standing and untouched by fire. I kept going, not sure where I was going to end up. People ignored me, as they mostly did anyway. I couldn't help wonder how Samuel Pepys was, or Jane in all this chaos as I continued my journey. Eventually I ended up here, Parliament Hill. I have been here ever since and don't know where else to go, at least until the fires die down. I am then determined to find Jane again and live with her. With that, Chester sat down, his tail flicking slowly from side to side. He wiped a tear away with his paw as he thought of Jane and what had become of her. All three sat for a long while in silence as dawn began to break over the devastated city of London.

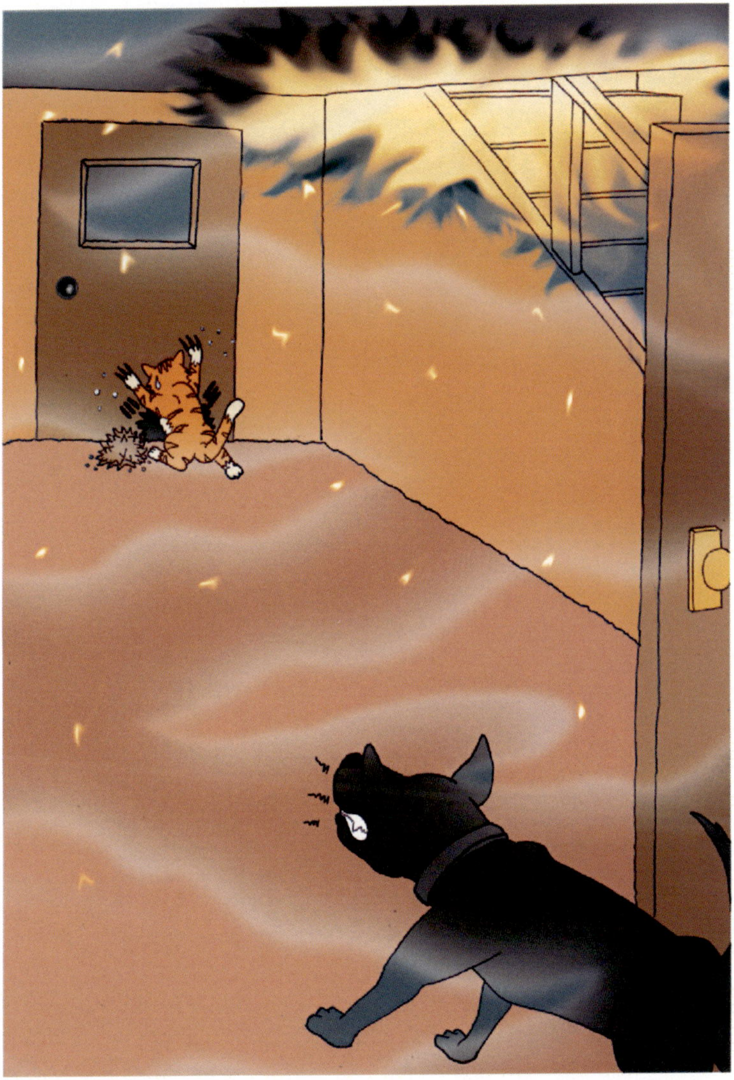

Sally's Story

The calm before the storm

It was looking like it was going to be another hot, sunny day in London but the sun didn't seem to warm the three friends up too much. A chill ran through them as they continued to watch the fire from Parliament Hill.

"It seems to be dying down a little, there isn't as much smoke rising up now", acknowledged Chester to the others.

"At last, it must be ending by now, surely?" Harry hoped and prayed that it would soon finish and they could all get back to their lives. And now they turned, both Harry and Chester, to Sally.

"Come on Sally, it's your turn now. Tell us how you came to be up here. How did the fire affect you these past few days?" With that, Sally stretched her aching muscles, stood up and began her story of escaping the greatest fire of all.

"I loved living in the Cathedral and the surrounding houses as there was so much going on. There were so many books to read that it would take me a thousand rat lifetimes to get through them all. I spent many a day, not in the Cathedral, but down the road in St Paul's school. Here there were all the books I could possibly want to read.

"You are clever Sally. I can't read a thing, never been taught!"

"I had a very good teacher, my Mother. I shouldn't worry Chester, a lot of people can't, let alone the likes of us!"

"Anyhow, I had heard about the fire and that it was creeping towards me. The talk amongst the people was that it wouldn't get to the Cathedral. Everyone was so confident of this that they had started to put their goods, along with books and manuscripts, into the vault under the Cathedral for safekeeping. I wanted to keep out of everyone's way so spent a lot of time in the school.

"This was where it all started, all the terrible events that I will never ever forget. I was reading in the library at St Paul's school, engrossed in a book as I usually was, when I heard a scream from outside. I put the book down and ran to the window to look at the commotion.

"Was it the fire, Sally? I bet it was the fire that you saw!"

"Shush, Chester. Sally is telling the story, not you". Harry silenced Chester and waited for Sally to explain.

"Yes, Chester is right. I looked out the window and a short way down the street saw billowing black smoke and a raging fire. It was spreading fast from house to house and heading straight for the school. Almost at once I could smell the smoke and knew the wind was blowing it straight towards me. I had to act.

"Knowing the Cathedral was the safest place (or so I thought) I ran out of the library. People in the school were running about, panicking. I didn't bother creeping about as I usually did but ran straight down the corridor until I got to the open window where I usually entered the school. I leapt up onto the sill (I can leap quite far when I have to) and scuttled down the stone of the School. I was faced with chaos. There were people screaming and running about. A number of carts were being pulled by people up and down the street. Horses were pulling more carts away from the spreading fire. I could see the birds fleeing the fire, spiralling up and up through the smoke into the clear blue sky. I felt the heat of the fire as it approached the school as I turned and ran to the Cathedral.

Hiding in the Tower

"I entered the Cathedral and ran up and up to my home in the Tower, passing people who were huddled together, confident that they had escaped the fire. Once in the tower I relaxed a bit. I was, after all, home. I went over to the small window from where I could see far and wide. To my dismay, the school was no more. The flames had consumed it and I could see the stones were crumbling and the roof had completely caved in.

"I am so glad you ran when you did Sally. You wouldn't have stood a chance in the school". Chester had said what they all were thinking, none more so than Sally herself.

"It wasn't only the school; all of Paternoster Row, Carter Lane, Ludgate Hill and Fleet Street were well ablaze. All these streets circled the Cathedral, trapping us all inside. Surely the flames wouldn't reach the Cathedral? I could feel the heat of the fire and taste the smoke in the air. Looking down I could see that there wasn't anywhere for the fire to take hold. The Cathedral was built of heavy stone which I knew wouldn't catch fire. I felt relieved after seeing this until I looked into the air.

"What did you see, Sally?"

"I saw my worst fear Harry, my very worst fear". Sally shook her head slowly as she recalled the events that followed.

"There were burning embers that rose up in the smoke and

some were settling on the wooden scaffolding that was supporting the very tower I was hiding in. I saw several pieces smouldering and knew that they would catch if left. I clambered out onto the scaffold and made my way to the burning embers. They were too hot to pick up so I tried blowing them out. I also used my tail to swipe at them and managed to dislodge some but more and more appeared and soon there was far too many for a little rat to cope with. The scaffold erupted in flame and I only just made it back to the tower window as bit by bit it collapsed, falling to the street below. At this point I noticed the roof had also caught fire, burning brightly in the sunshine.

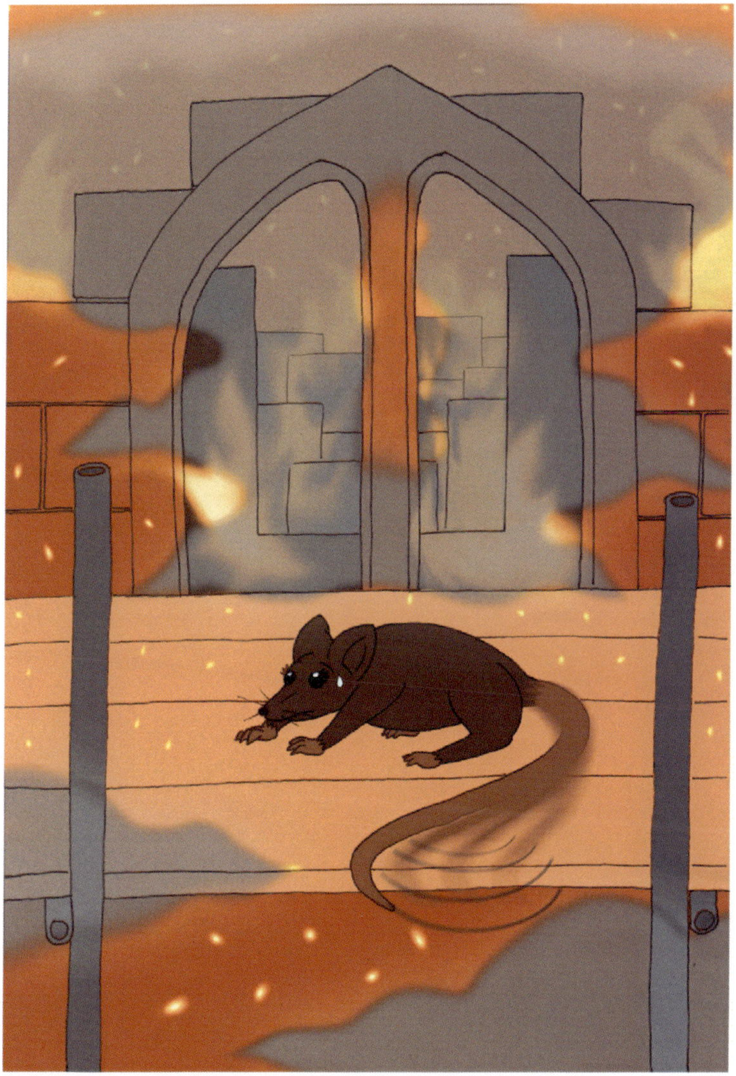

The Molten River

"I could feel the heat of the fire on the roof and heard an awful cracking noise as the roof split straight across, bits of stone rained down and I had to dodge them as I ran to the stairs. Then I heard the sound of water.

"Water could put out the fire, Sally. Did it save the Cathedral?" Chester had his paws crossed, hoping that this story would end happily, unlike his and Harry's. Sadly, he was going to be disappointed.

"The sound was like water, but it wasn't water that I saw. It was the lead roof that had melted and was spilling into the room. A tiny bit splashed onto my paw as it hit the floor. With that, Sally held her paw aloft to reveal a little burn mark. Sally continued. It was very hot and would kill anything it touched. I turned my tail and ran down the stairs. I could hear the gushing lead following me, getting closer and closer. Looking back I could see the molten river cascading over the steps and gaining, gaining, gaining. I knew that I couldn't outrun the deadly river and just as it was about to consume me I leapt as high as I could from one of the steps at the bottom of the tower.

"Where did you land Sally? How did you escape the molten river?" Sally had completely engrossed Chester and Harry who were desperate to know how she survived.

"As I have told you before, I can leap quite high and far

when I need to, and this was one of those times. I managed to grab the bottom of a wall tapestry as I jumped and clung on as the swirling, molten lead flowed beneath me. I clambered up to the top of the tapestry until the lead had all flowed past. I then cautiously climbed down and continued into the main part of the Cathedral.

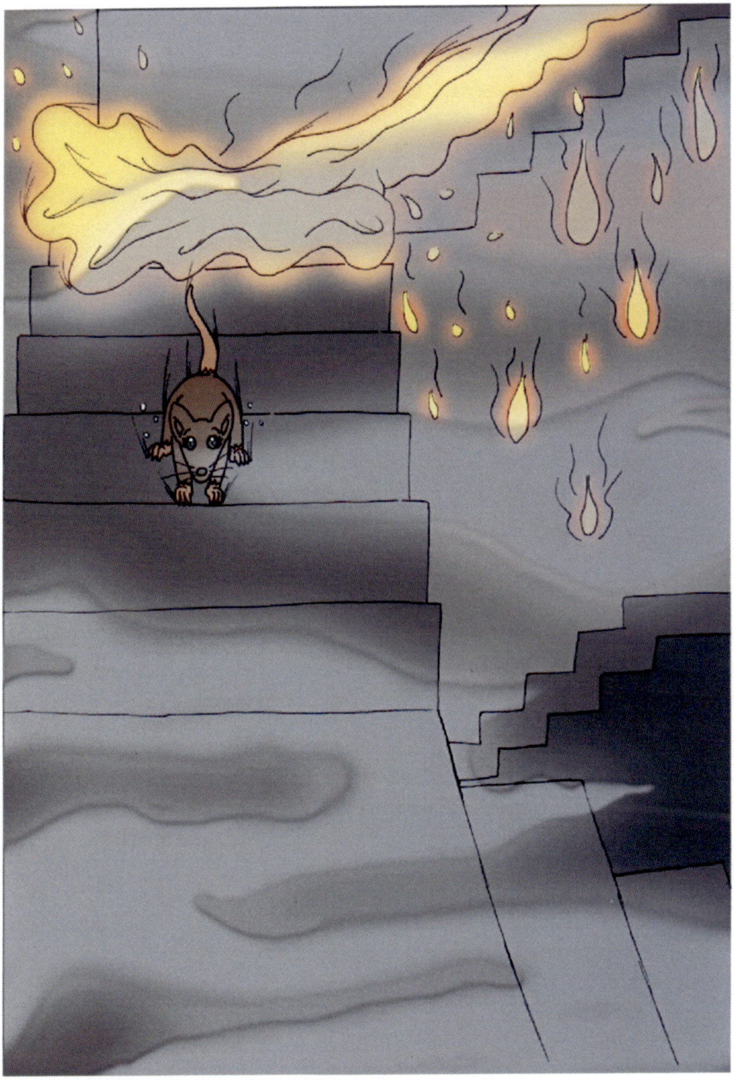

Look out below!

"I didn't have time to draw breath and count myself lucky that I didn't get consumed by the molten river as I heard a series of loud bangs and crashes above me.

"What was it Sally? Could you see what it was?" Harry was itching to know what was making the noise.

"Well, looking up I could certainly see what the banging was. Through the smoke and flames I could see large stones falling down into the Nave from the very ceiling itself. The Cathedral was collapsing around me. I remember one large stone crashed right next to me and bounce down the centre of the Cathedral. People nearby were running screaming from the building and I wasn't going to hang around myself. It may have been my home all my life but I wasn't about to let it become my tomb!

"I ran, dodging and weaving the falling stones as I went first one way, then the other until I could see the door to the Cathedral ahead of me. I was almost there when a huge piece of stone dropped right in front of the door. It completely blocked my path! I was trapped. Smoke, fire and falling stones were my only companions, along with one old woman who was cowering in the corner of the transept. I knew it was only a matter of time before the Cathedral was completely destroyed. I had to get out!

"Please tell us how you escaped Sally; I don't think I can take any more of this". Harry had a very worried look on his face and was clearly scared for Sally's predicament. Sally was keen to finish the story, especially as the memories were making her scared too.

"Ok, well, as I tried to hide in the South Transept the roof gave way completely and a surge of the remaining molten lead poured into the Nave, covering everything it touched with red hot liquid. I noticed one of the great windows had been smashed to smithereens by the large stones from the roof and I sprinted towards it. I jumped onto a fallen stone, then another and then another. Each leap got me closer and closer to the window. I could smell the air from the street outside and I knew one more leap would see me out. There was molten lead dripping down in front of the window but I had no time to wait to see if it would stop. The flames and smoke were making it so difficult to breathe that I knew I had only a few seconds left. I leapt as high as I could and jumped over the edge of the window, down onto the street below.

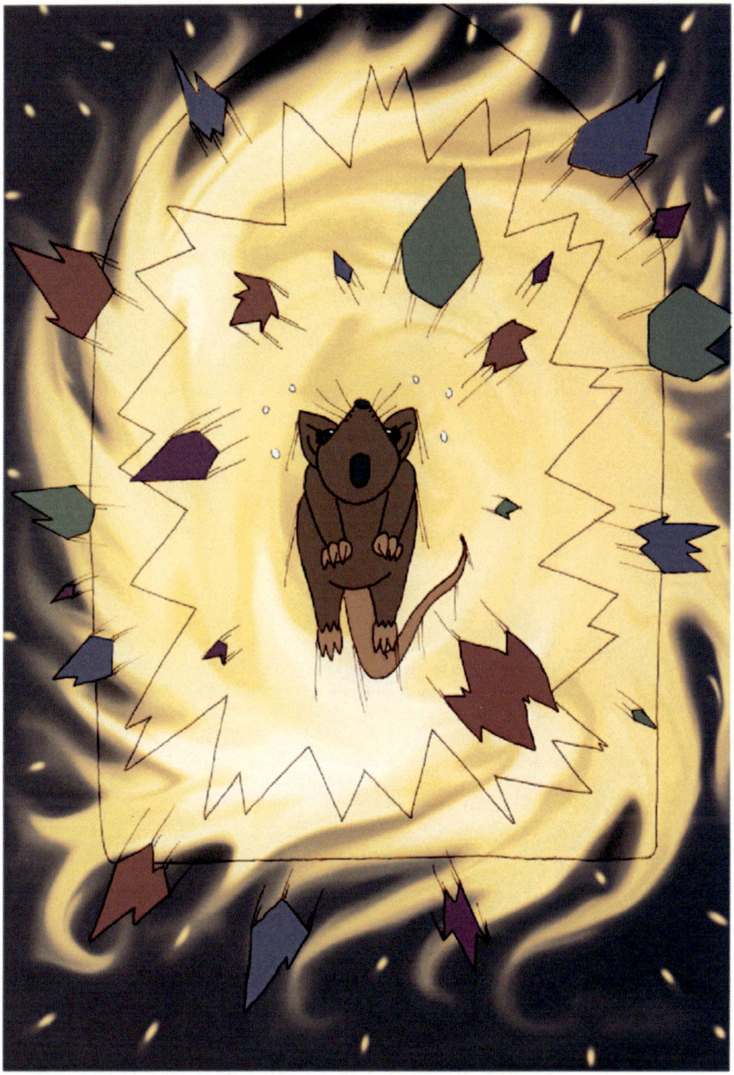

Horse play!

"St Paul's was in ruins. The roof had gone, and now in the Nave the walls were beginning to fall inwards. My home for so long was gone forever. I couldn't watch the devastation for long though of course. I had made it out of the Cathedral in one piece but still had to escape the city. There was fire everywhere, I was surrounded. All the buildings were ablaze and I couldn't see a way to run without falling foul of smoke or fire.

"Get on a passing cart, Sally. It's the best way to get about London quickly".

"It is so long as the people don't see you. I doubt they would be too friendly towards you. Mice and rats have never been as popular as cats and dogs you know, Chester". Harry was right of course. People were more inclined to try to squish a rat than to help them. Of this, Sally was all too aware.

"I knew that I had to be careful where people were concerned but my only saving grace was that they were all more worried about the fire than a little rat scurrying by. I looked for a cart to clamber onto but there were none. Most people had fled before the fire became too bad. I was beginning to run out of ideas, when I head a loud whinny behind me.

"Turning round I saw a large cart horse, minus the cart, galloping toward me. It was big enough to leap over the flames and through the smoke but was clearly scared. All at once I saw my way out. If I could somehow leap onto the horse as it passed I would be able to ride out of the Cathedral grounds without succumbing to the raging fires.

"Have you ever tried to jump onto a moving horse, Sally? I imagine it's quite scary and very hard to do!" Harry shook his little head in bewilderment and Chester nodded in agreement too.

"It's not something I would usually do but these were desperate times and I had little choice. Jump for safety or burn in the fire.

"What a choice to have to make. I guess anything is worth a try in that situation", remarked Harry and of course he was absolutely right.

"The horse was running up to the flames then stopping, then backing off and running again. I could see he was plucking up the courage to jump over and I had to be ready when he did. I scrambled onto a large stone that had once been part of the Cathedral wall. From here I reckoned that I would have a good chance of successfully jumping onto the horse's back, or so I thought!

As the horse ran past me for a third time I could see he was going to finally jump over the flames into the street beyond. He stopped, turned around and with a large whinny, galloped towards the flames. He was getting closer and closer and I knew I had to time my jump to perfection. When the horse was almost by me I jumped, high into the air. I could see the horse galloping past me; see his brown mane and back. Then I was falling but to my horror realised I had jumped too late! He was galloping so fast I thought for one dreadful moment that I had missed him completely!

Clinging by a thread

"I reached out with my paws as I landed on the horse's lower back. I tried to grab onto the horse but his hair was so short that I just slid, down and down until I slipped off the end of the horse. My saving grace was his long black tail that I just managed to grab before I hit the floor. There I was swinging on the end of the horse's tail for the entire world to see.

"The horse had obviously noticed what had happened and whinnied to me to "hold on tight" as he leapt high into the air. I could see the flames below me, feel their heat and taste the foul smoke. For a moment I couldn't see anything and it seemed that the whole world had fallen silent as we flew through the air. This seemed to take an age but finally we hit the cobbled street with a clatter. The horse skidded but managed to keep on his feet. After that he trotted further up the street until the flames and smoke receded. We had made it!

"Oh Sally, that is probably the BRAVEST thing of all of us. Imagine riding a horse to escape the fire, unbelievable". Harry and Chester were both really proud of Sally for what she had done. Sally just blushed and continued her story!

"I thanked the horse for saving my life, albeit unknowingly! He said us animals should stick together in times like these and told me his name was Chestnut. I clambered up onto his back and held onto his thick, black mane. Chestnut and I walked up the streets away from the fire. Several people stared in disbelief when they saw me sitting on Chestnut but I didn't care any more. I was just glad that we had escaped and everything was all right. We kept walking until we arrived at Parliament Hill. Chestnut said I would be safe here and wished me well. He was heading up to Oxford, a place far away from London where he was born. I wished him luck too. I hope he made it!

Sally sat back down, her story told. All three fell silent as they thought of the dangers and adventures that had befallen them all over the past few days. All three knew that they were very lucky to have escaped the worst fire in London's history.

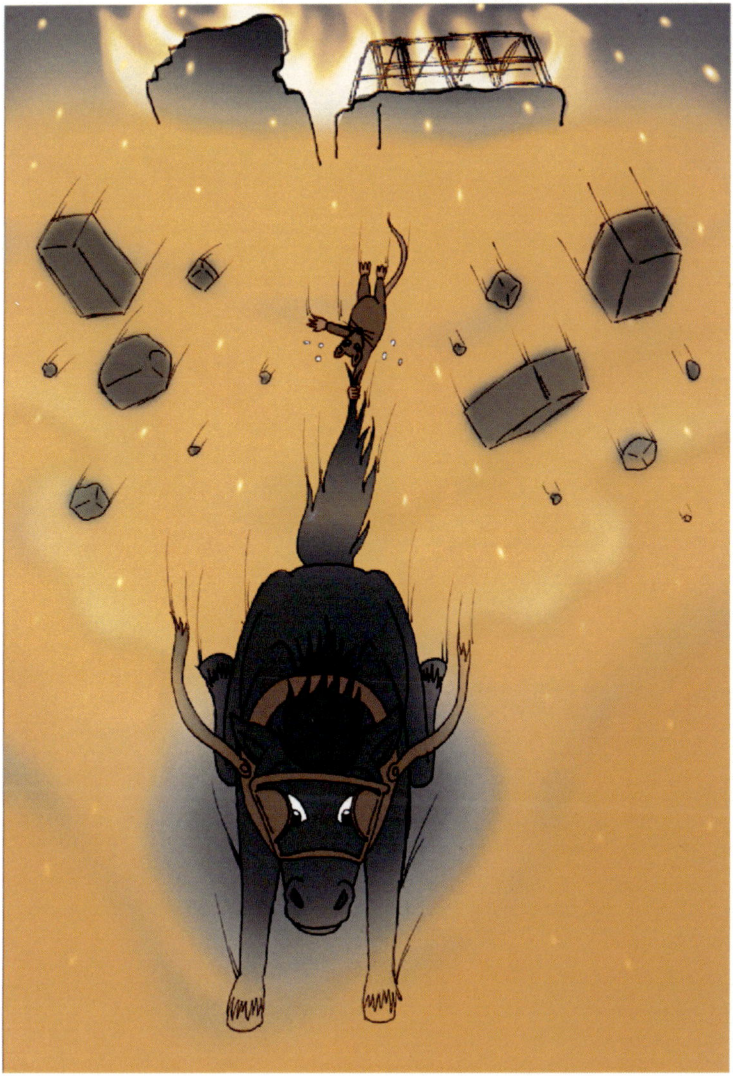

The end of it all

Over the next few days the three stayed together on the hill. They slept up against an old tree which overlooked the city. They watched the comings and goings of the people and saw the fire dying down and finally going out, although there were small fires that burned for many days to come.

All were becoming increasingly keen to return to the city to see how their homes had fared.

"The fires have died down, people are returning to London. Let's go and see how it is?" suggested Sally to her two friends who both nodded in agreement and so together they set off for the city.

Harry, Chester and Sally hitched a ride on a horse drawn cart that was heading back into London. No one saw them as they sneaked under the old rug on the back of the cart. Chester, being the tallest, got on first and helped the other two to climb aboard. They peered out on the journey and saw the devastation that had befallen the city. Houses were reduced to rubble, fires still burned here and there. People were still trying to put them out but the damage had already been done. The trio got off at St Paul's Cathedral, Sally's home. They couldn't believe what they saw!

The ruined Cathedral

The three small animals looked at the Cathedral in disbelief. The once so grand and beautiful building had been reduced to rubble. The lead roof that had chased Sally was now hard and created a blanket of lead over some of the stone. Most of the walls had tumbled down and you could see into what was once the great Nave. Altars were smashed, windows destroyed.

Even the floor of the Cathedral was ruined. It was cracked and smashed. Some of the coffins buried in the floor had been upturned and exposed. There were indeed, several people standing around one such coffin examining the dead body that lay within. St Paul's cathedral was nothing more than a shell of a building now.

As they cautiously walked around the building, Chester let out a sudden gasp of horror and pointed to a place a few paces in front of them. There was a body of an old lady who had obviously gone to the Cathedral to seek shelter from the fire. It hadn't saved her. Her body was blackened and twisted from the heat of the fire. It must have been a terrible end for the woman. All three animals fell silent at the sight of the old woman until they had walked past.

"It's gone, all gone. What am I going to do now? Where on earth am I going to live?" sobbed Sally in desperation.

"Don't worry Sally. You have us as friends now. Stick with

us and you will be just fine". Harry's words of friendship encouraged Sally. Maybe things weren't as bad as she had thought! At least they were alive and well. With this thought in mind, all three continued on into the city.

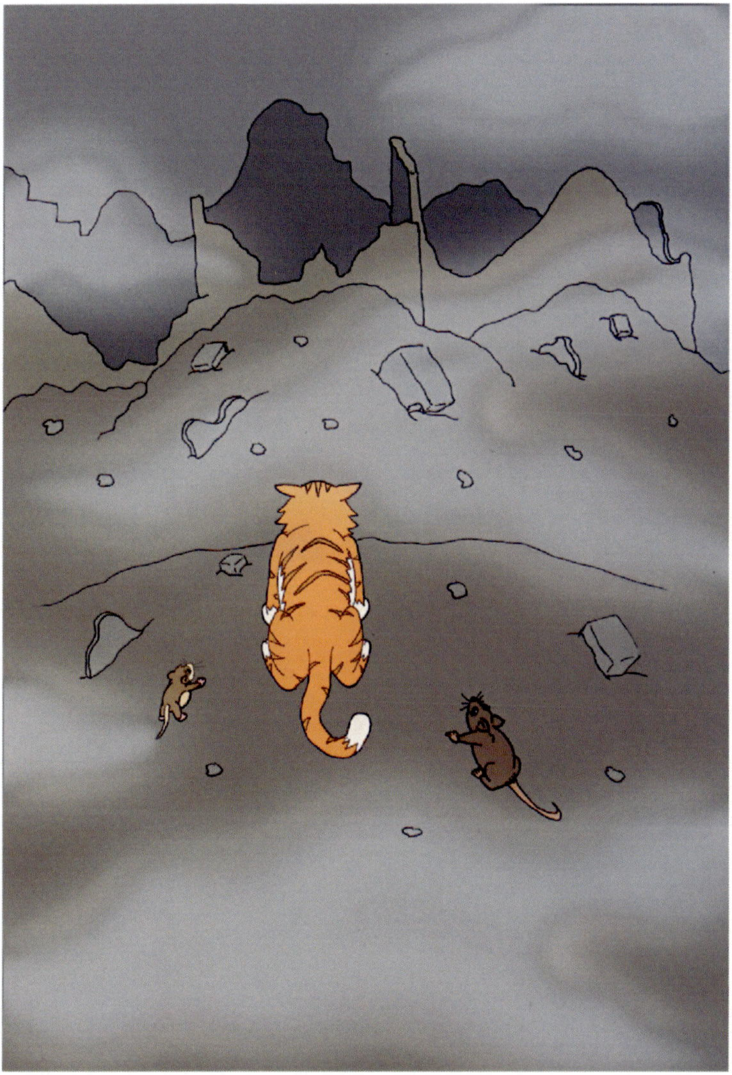

A friendly face

Picking their way carefully through the devastated streets, the three companions continued on, unsure of where they were going but just glad that they were going there together. The streets were so unrecognisable that Harry almost missed the ruin of the Mayor's house where he had almost met his end.

"Here's the Mayor's house. Can you believe I actually survived that?" remarked Harry, looking at the charred rubble that lay all around.

"You were lucky Harry, so very lucky".

"I agree with you Chester, a lucky escape indeed", said Sally looking at the remains of the house. As she was looking, something colourful caught her eye.

"Oh look, both of you. What a beautiful bird there is on that stone over there!"

Both looked over and Harry gasped in astonishment. It was the bird he had rescued from that very house! Harry called up to the bird who was so surprised to see Harry that he almost fell off the stone he was perched on.

"You escaped! Oh thank you, thank you. I can't tell you how grateful I am to you for rescuing me from the fire. I never even caught your name!" The bird was so happy to see Harry and they chatted for ages about their good fortune. It seemed that the bird was planning on flying south over the sea to seek a new home. They all bid farewell and wished him luck in finding a new home. Harry was so pleased and swelled with pride at getting so much attention!

Harry decided not to go to Pudding Lane. He couldn't face seeing the ruin of his much loved home as it would only upset him. The others agreed but none knew where they should go. Chester suddenly had an idea.

"Let's go to my home. It may well be burned but if we can find Jane, we could go home with her. I am sure that she will sort things out for us".

They all agreed that it was a very good plan and slowly made their way through the city to Samuel Pepys' house. As they travelled the streets became busier and busier with people trying to salvage any possessions that they could find. The animals slunk into the shadows to avoid being seen.

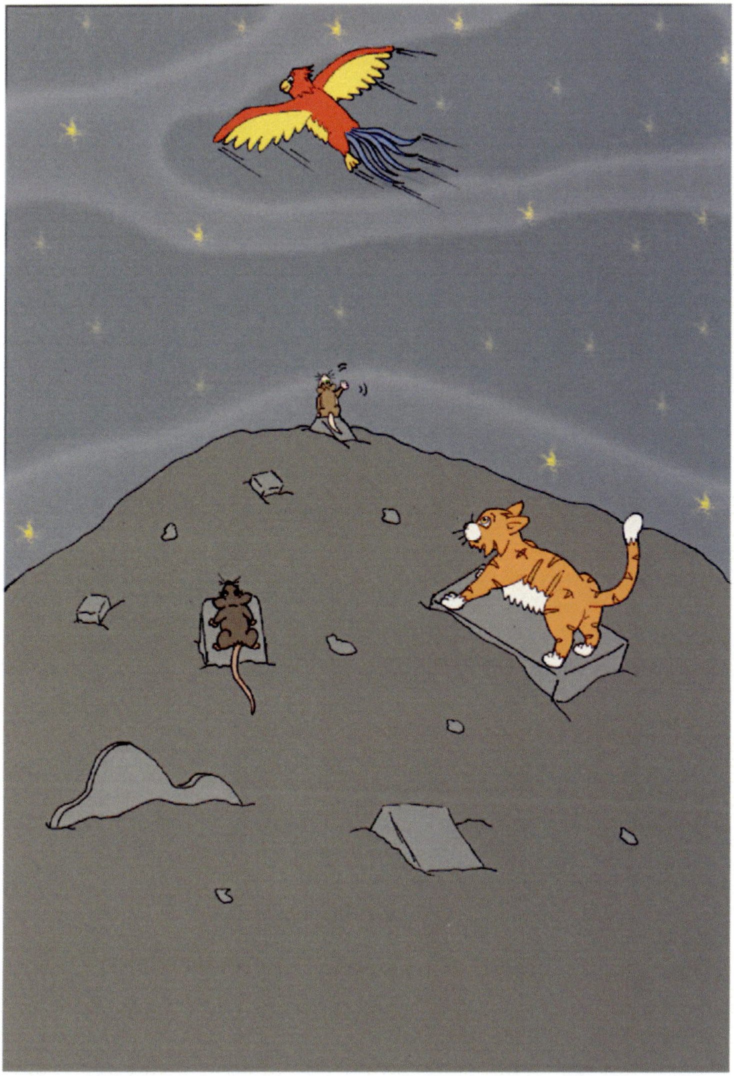

A home at last

Finally they arrived at Chester's house. As he had feared, the fire had spread this far and the house had been destroyed. Sally and Harry comforted Chester as best they could who was surprisingly chipper considering! The two smaller animals stayed at Samuel Pepys' house as Chester continued up the street looking for Jane. He climbed on piles of rubble and loudly called her name. He walked up the street and down the street and was beginning to lose hope when all at once he spied her! She was walking to the remains of the house and couldn't believe Chester was alive and well.

"Oh my little pussy cat, however did you survive? I am so pleased to see you!" And with that she picked Chester up in her arms and cuddled him so tight that he thought he may stop breathing! Harry and Sally beamed with pleasure when they saw Chester being carried down the street towards them. He had found Jane for sure!

Chester, Harry and Sally left the city with Jane in the back of a cart drawn by a large grey pony. Well, Harry and Sally travelled in secret at the back but not for Chester this time. Oh no, Chester sat proudly in the front with Jane, telling her all the adventures he and his new friends had been through. Not that she could understand of course but she seemed happy to hear Chester purring so much!

They made their way from London, travelling on dusty

roads that had similar carts coming and going and all laden with belongings. They eventually came to Oxford. Jane had relatives who were kind enough to let her live with them in return for her to do the housework and chores for them. And they welcomed Chester with open arms!

Sally made her home in a nearby church and was content in her steeple overlooking the town. It wasn't anywhere near as big as St Paul's but was still a lovely place to live. She soon made friends with all the other rats living nearby who loved to hear the adventures of Sally and her friends.

Harry missed the baker and his little home near the ovens in Pudding Lane. He lived in the same house as Chester and made a home under the floorboards of the main dining room. He was always careful not to be seen and had a plentiful supply of food. Scraps from the kitchen and things Chester brought for him.

It was only Harry who made the journey back to London, and then only once, He had to find out what happened to his family who had headed for the bridge on the night the fire broke out. Harry saw the city being rebuilt as he headed to the South side. The bridge had burned only half way, saved by a gap in the houses. To his immense relief he found his family safe and well at his cousin's house. They had made it before the fire had consumed the bridge. Harry invited his family to visit him in Oxford, an invitation they took up a few weeks later.

London had taken a pounding from the fire. Over two thirds had been destroyed and it would take many years, and a lot of planning to make the city great again. Over time, it returned to being the greatest city in England.

Chester, Harry and Sally loved their new homes in Oxford and settled in to a peaceful life, away from the hustle and bustle of the big city. But the best thing of all about living in Oxford was the fact that they could see each other whenever they liked.

All three knew how lucky they had been not to perish in the Great Fire of London and, even luckier, to have found such good friends.

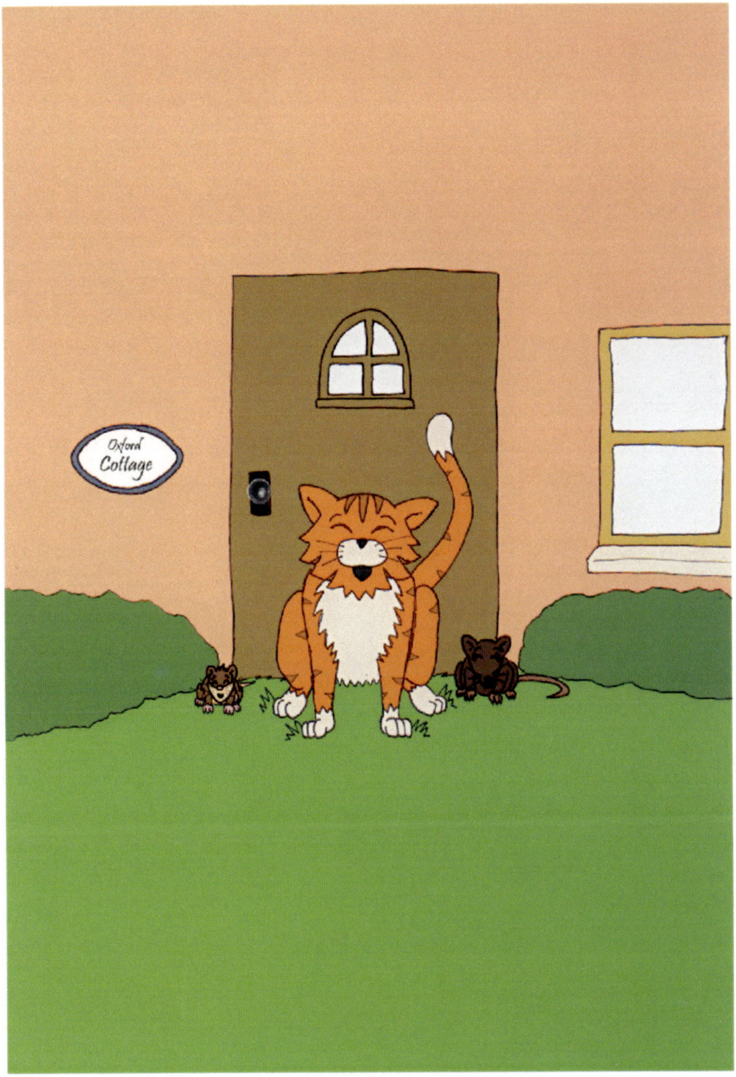
Oxford
Cottage